For Barbara, thank you for your friendship and support
~ GR

For Rosemary
~ SM

First published in 2011 by Scholastic Children's Books
Euston House, 24 Eversholt Street
London NW1 1DB
a division of Scholastic Ltd
www.scholastic.co.uk
London ~ New York ~ Toronto ~ Sydney ~ Auckland
Mexico City ~ New Delhi ~ Hong Kong

HB ISBN 978 1407 12454 4
PB ISBN 978 1407 12907 5

You Can't Scare a Princess!

Written by
Gillian Rogerson

Illustrated by
Sarah McIntyre

Princess Spaghetti was teaching King Cupcake how to roller skate when they saw a ship sailing up the Royal Moat.

"Look, Father – pirates!"
said Princess Spaghetti.

"Oooh, yippee!" cheered King Cupcake, as he skated towards the ship.

"Be careful!" Princess Spaghetti warned,
as she scooted after him.
Too late. King Cupcake was tied up!
"Oh dear!" he sighed.

"Arrrrrrr!" bellowed the pirate captain. "I'm Captain Waffle, the meanest, baddest pirate in the whole wide world!"

Captain Waffle waved a map at the princess. "There is treasure in these parts – and you're going to help me find it."

The pirates searched the palace from top to bottom.
"Do you have to make such a **mess**?"
Princess Spaghetti said crossly.

The treasure was nowhere to be found.

"Let me look at the map," Princess Spaghetti said.

"Keep your princess fingers off!" Captain Waffle sulked.

"Do you want to find the treasure or not?" Princess Spaghetti said as she took the map. **"It's upside down!** The treasure is buried in the garden – we'll need to be up high to see it."

Princess Spaghetti led the pirates to the Royal Hot Air Balloon.

"Come on, jump in."

The pirates climbed into the basket, but the balloon didn't move.

"You're too heavy, you'll
have to leave your things behind,"
Princess Spaghetti told them.

The Royal Hot Air Balloon floated high above Cupcake Palace. "Over there!" Princess Spaghetti pointed.

Captain Waffle grabbed the controls.
"Prepare for landing, shipmates!"
"Watch out for the tree!"
yelled Princess Spaghetti,
covering her eyes.

CRASH!

"Now what?" Captain Waffle wailed.
"Now we make a rope out of your
headscarves and climb down,"
said Princess Spaghetti.

Captain Waffle looked worried.
"That sounds dangerous."
The princess smiled. "I'll go first."

When they reached the
ground, they began to dig.

Down,

down,

down. Until ...

"It's not fair! That Captain Nastybeard always pinches my treasure!" Captain Waffle tore up the map, threw it on the ground and stamped on it.

The rest of the crew began to cry.
"I want my treasure!"
"I want to go home!"
"I want my mummy!"

"There, there," said Princess Spaghetti. "You know, you really should give up stealing treasure. Roller skating is **much** more fun. Untie my father and I'll show you how to do it."

"Well, shiver me timbers!"
Captain Waffle chuckled.
"This IS fun!"

It was time for the pirates to go home.

"Take the roller skates with you," Princess Spaghetti said.

"And remember, skating is more fun than stealing!"

"Ay ay, Princess." Captain Waffle grinned.

Then he turned to his crew and winked.

"And **skating** will make **stealing**

a whole lot more fun. Look out,

Captain Nastybeard. **Arrrrr!**"

The End